My Big Book of the Outdoors

By JANE WERNER WATSON
Illustrated by ELOISE WILKIN

A GOLDEN BOOK, NEW YORK
Western Publishing Company, Inc., Racine, Wisconsin 53404

Library of Congress Catalog Card Number: 82-82713 ISBN 0-307-11405-8/ISBN 0-307-60406-3 (lib. bdg.)
B C D E F G H I J

This book was originally published as WONDERS OF NATURE.

Did you know
that the woods can tell
that spring is coming
before the snow is gone?

The sleeping plants
send up green shoots.
And the tree buds
swell and open.

Did you know
that some seeds
have wings . . .

maple

and some have
tiny silken
parachutes,

dandelion

and some seeds
are hidden away
in fruits . . .

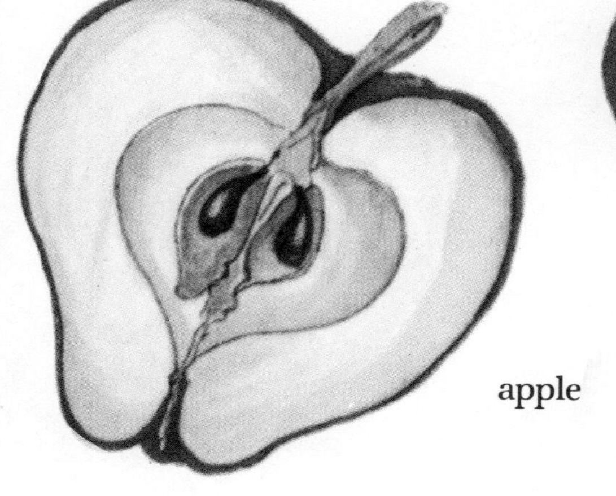

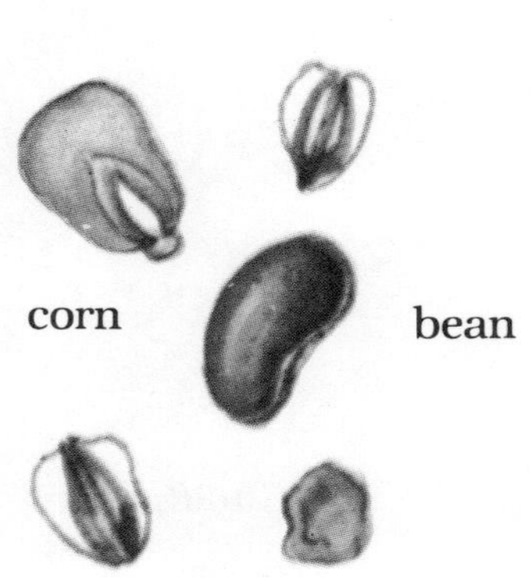

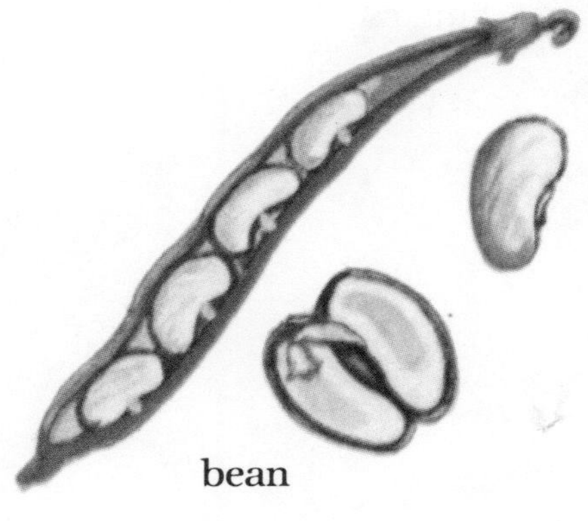

and that every seed,
no matter how tiny,
has a whole tiny plant
inside, with food to use
when it starts to grow?

Did you know
that tiny coral animals
under the sea,
which never move,
build big towers
and islands
of their tiny shells?

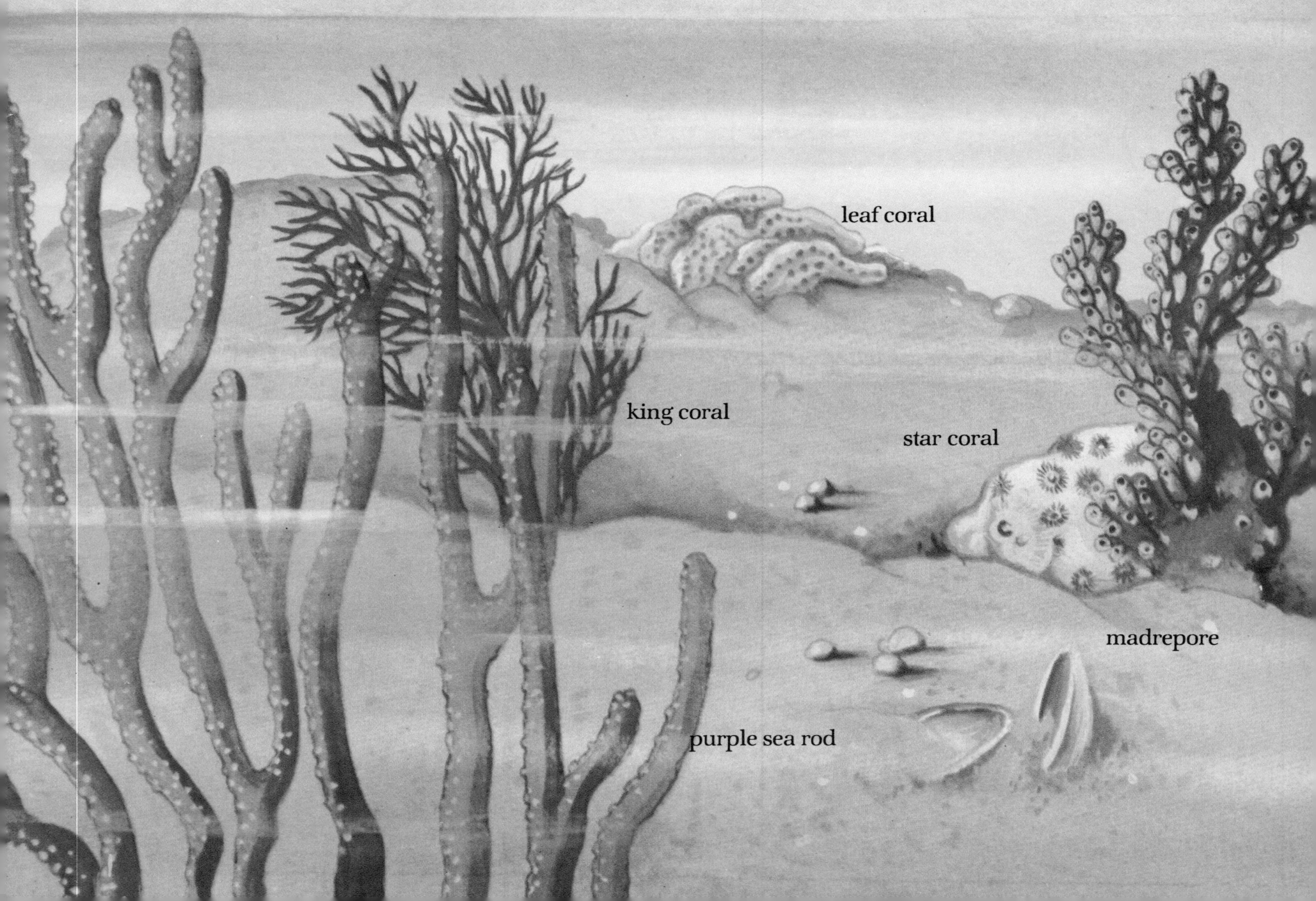

leaf coral

king coral

star coral

madrepore

purple sea rod

organ-pipe coral
brain coral

Did you know
that in the dry desert
some plants have thick stems
in which they store water,
and lots of prickly spines
to keep thirsty animals
from eating them up?

And the kangaroo rat
who lives in the desert
never drinks water,
but makes it in its body
out of crisp, dry seeds.

Did you know
that the beaver
can chew through a young tree
in just a few minutes?

He bites off the branches and uses them
to build a dam across a stream.

And all the birds around,
and the squirrels and opossums,
the rabbits and the chipmunks,
the deer and the moose,
enjoy that beaver pond.

Did you know
that far up north
in the land of ice and snow
we call the Arctic,

animals have winter coats
of fur as white as the snow?

Did you know that some birds fly
thousands of miles over ocean and land . . .

then come back to the same special spots
to lay their eggs?

And that salmon swim
hundreds of miles to shore
and far up the rivers
and over the waterfalls . . .

to come back to their special spots
to lay their eggs?

Did you know
that fireflies
have lights in their bodies
they can flash on and off . . .

and that crickets "chirp" by rubbing
their wings together?

Did you know
that some fish
in the deep, dark ocean
have little lights
along their sides
or dangling in front
of their noses?

lanternfish

angler

firefly fish

Did you know
that out in the pond
smooth wiggly tadpoles
lose their tails and grow legs,
and turn into frogs?

And that fuzzy caterpillars
weave silken cocoons
around themselves
and go to sleep,
then wake up as pretty moths
or butterflies?

And did you know
that all of nature's wonders
are everywhere around you
in the big outdoors?